Mornings

Robert Renard

ISBN: 9781792665134

DEDICATION

To Reanne, my lover, friend and fellow traveler.

CONTENTS

ACKNOWLEDGMENTS

I want to thank the many members of my writer's group who over the years
have supported and given my words attention and love. Without their
tenderness I would have been orphaned in the world of literature.
Instead my soul has been nurtured
and helped to heal.

New Years Day

Making soup
using a new recipe
is the answer
so as not to stew about things.

Edge

I place it on the edge
just in time
a matter of space
before.

In that in-between place
just as then becomes
after.

I must wait to see
just what comes
next.

Noticing

The words too fast
or an unfamiliar topic
unable to keep up
or just not interested
I notice
the conversations
are changing.

I am familiar
with the history
listening with half an ear
about places and times
I do not know
never will
but lately the here and now
events of others' lives
the small talk of the day
is largely lost on me.

My mom would say
*...if you can't remember
forget it!*
a cute phrase
turned out to be
the first sign
of her decline
she really could not remember
so fear sparks
in my brain now.

I find myself
wondering is this the start
the conversation missed
like a streetcar
passing me by
while others easily jump aboard
and enjoy the ride.

I yearn to join the ride
so try harder
hoping it will help me
but I also wonder
would not my mother have noticed
so did she try harder too?

No rush

I unload the dishwasher
feed the dogs
refill empty containers
clean the sink
dust and straighten
the chores of the day
now transformed
what I do
retirement's gift.

It is mostly easy
days flow
the clock too
life seems to have found
a slower pace
rushing has become
out of the ordinary
retirement's gift.

Working less
means playing more
writing often
when I choose
nothing drives me
nuts have become a snack
not a state of mind
retirement's gift.

Really looking
towards a future
this seeking births plans
instead of necessity
wrapped in desperation
this is retirement's best gift.

Rewrites

Do I rewrite my poems
or do they rewrite me?

If they are my scripture
then as the Sages taught
the lines of words
reveal a future
teaching me
like dreams
to become more
something better.

Partly cloudy

Gloomy
with a chance of showers
the report
tears from my heart
in the forecast.

Finding lost notes

No longer
the ones from work
or the to do list
not where to go
and when.

It is my fingers
that seem to have forgotten
the sharps and flats
on my saxophone
my ears remember
noticing what is lost
hoping
we can find them.

Honored

He asked me
if it bothered me
his requests for help
my reply surprised him
I was honored.

Asking a sign of our friendship
the bond between us
he trusts me
and believes I have something
to offer him
this is never a bother
it is an honor.

We went on
sharing asking seeking
reassurance the unspoken
connection between us
as we soaked in
the caring and respect
and the honor.

Recycled

The final day's chess match
signaled our transition
the tattered chessboard
discarded
followed by each piece in turn
carefully placed in the bin
even the precious knights
with their broken legs
never put out of their misery
instead held together
scotch taped on their bases
for five years now
finally put out to pasture
recycled
like us
to something different
something new.

Kind words

Often saying little
or nothing
we are taught
is the correct thing to do
usually it is
where kindness dwells.

Children waiting

Thin words whispered
from young tongues
sometimes careful
most times carefree
now angry and desperate
demanding more
expressed through lips
shouting
high up on tippy-toes
marching in the streets
where we should join them.

Achilles

My heel reminds me
like Achilles
weakness is a part of life
a limp can be healed
so what one does in life
to overcome
is what makes it worthwhile.

Tick tock

My ticker needed graphing
I mistakenly chose
the left side
where they don't know me
the slow side of the office
the tick tock on the wall
later and later
the mistaken medical orders
the lack of sincerity
no caring in the medical suite
soured me
my ticker was angry.

My chest shaved
without a word
they figured I would know
no doubt
the contacts found faulty
reattached twice
still my cardio did not diagram
my ticker was angry.

Third time the charm
Hannah to the rescue
arriving in the nick
from the right side
my doctor's side of the office
she dotted all the i's
crossed all the t's
to help me out of my pinch
she did the graph
I was on my way
my ticker was happy.

Least Heat Moon

Going out
the four directions his guide
with no place in mind
finding himself in places
that gives opportunities
he must decide
to grasp hold
with curiosity
to notice
and pay attention
to reap the bounty of being
present in that one moment
finding peace.

Eighth day post-surgery

First there was
pain from the cut
the scraping away
body's repair job
its attempt to protect my Achilles
became more trouble
the pain signaled more
had to be done
so pain after cut
is worthwhile.

The surgeon's blade
renews my heel
back to its original
intended nature
the operation seeks
to repair my world
to heal a piece
broken.

Now day eight
heralds more pain
most passes quickly
like a change of mind
then there is are the sharp jabs
followed by dull aches
but worst of all
the hot throbs that settle in
visiting too long
like an unwelcomed guest.

I will rest a bit today
and focus
on friends and future
adding these
gives me a new sense
rest and renewal
on this eighth day
as my life continues
improved.

Happiness

Move?
they say am crazy
to leave this place.

To their disbelieving ears
I say
I must
to find happiness
and peace.

Going out

I want to study with a friend
to enrich our lives
and reduce my loneliness
the Sages understood
it was the way
even the wise old fool
had a companion
so where is mine?
will they appear
on the way?

I see my obstacle
fear
I have stopped
reaching out
stopped asking
staying too safe
on my way.

I must ask
again take the risk
like my relations
who's going out
brought me here
their faith enabled me
to come all
this way.

I must go out.

Murmur

My words have gone dry
or being held in my deep
the well where I once drew them
has lost its bucket
my fingers have lost their touch.

I am up this morning
trying to raise a note or two
hearing them within me
their echo remains
a murmur is all I hear.

I search for a way to lift
lacking a bucket, pencil or pen
I peck out what is on the surface
like moisture after a shower
it offers but a hint
of what still lies below
my deep whispers.

Seemed a good idea at the time

Off to the park
the dogs and I find
the entrance closed
round the long way we go
only to be stopped by the Edison crew
stop signs in hand
replacing their broken pole
followed by a lone workman
repairing the fence
crushed by the down pole.

Finally in the parking lot
the green so inviting
dogs leashed and at the ready
our walk underway
when a three-bladed mower
crosses our path
roaring in unison
with the whine of the chainsaws
punctuated by the falling branches
cymbal crashing to the ground
an overwhelming chorus
announcing the workmen's breaks are over
and so was mine.

Crumbs

We spoke of crumbs
that gathering them
may be in that moment
better than nothing.

Searching for a snack
serves our hunger
we are improved in that moment
but the hunger is not vanquished
it remains
gnawing on us.

And the gathering, it ends up
has eaten away at our self esteem
its bite reminds us
we are not good enough
we only deserve crumbs
so our hunger increases
and our desperation.

So we must be careful
our hollow spaces are sensitive
needing more than another crumb
a morsel we take in to satisfy the hunger
may sicken us later
leaving a bitter taste
worse than the gnawing.

Music to my ears

When she told me
that someday
we would walk out of our house
into the green
and see it all
my heart began sang
louder than a
a flock of birds
riot of chirps
shaking the still of a tree
the joyous gulp of the pelican's throat
full of pond fish
and the whippoorwill's whoop
always just out of sight.

I just wish

It is enough for now
wishes in the bright
walking hand in hand
a cool breeze on our cheeks
a warm sun all around
our future just ahead
waiting for us.

The passing

He passed by
a ghost in the mist of yesterdays
not noticing me there
moored at the ready
in the sea of pews
sails set
waiting for the wind.

I thought no
don't call out
he knows my depths
my charts could lead him
so I waited for the wind.

Words we had exchanged
I thought them enough
in the moment
my heart sank
until the wind
filled my sails
and righted my ship.

The days are changing

The days are changing
not in length
they are more
or less
somehow reflective
a mirror of my soul.

Steads they come
carrying me off
venturing still
into an unknown
less now than before.

A bed of soft
sweet scented honeysuckle
supporting me into safety
one never known
long lasting it has appeared
out of nowhere
the magic of this time.

The words come
from somewhere
not my mind
or my wisdom
as Jung believed
becoming universalized to something new
unimagined.

While my past is guarded
behind a veil
the deeper its hues become
as it transforms
my experience
so like my mother
I forget it since
I can't remember it.

Blending

The days are changing
blending so they cannot be captured
a texture that I can not be describe
so life becoming
quickening to some end
brought on not by the ticks of the clock
instead some new awareness
a glimmering twinkle
like stardust leavings
on a faint trail
which guides me on
step by step.

All

All reminds me
it takes me away
somewhere else
flashes in my mind's eye
at once I am there
wishing it was true.

Three notions on flowers

Thick masses of green wanes
magically topped by purple crowns
drift to and fro
in the late afternoon breeze.

Every fortnight
white with yellow centers
nature blooms
like clock work without gears.

They appear at night
sweet scented suckling
close to my window
sweetening my dreams.

Arising out of my garden
bringing to my senses
their sweet fragrance.

Moisture

My memories come
seeping out mostly
early in the cool quiet
when like other living things
I am still moist with dew.

 So what would I say
really that they would understand
needing more than they can give
an alien speaking
as though in tongues
so quietly
I must accept
not lose heart
and journey on
seeking a place
beyond.

They never ask

They wonder about my quiet
never asking
confirms my fears
and leaves me sadly
locked in a loneliness
of self-imposed
invisibility.

Workshop

I dream of a workshop
wide and full
made ready waiting
for my creativity to come
being older now
this need replaces others
lost mostly during the march of days
carved into my walking stick.

At loose ends

Between yesterday's memories
and next week's adventures
anticipation is readying me
while the space of now
a void
too wide appears
engulfing me.

Truth

Between the lines
is where the truth
is mostly found
like Torah
the white fire
completes the black.

Ordinary

Filled with morning's hope
I get dog food
mow the lawn
visit another car lot
bring in the garbage cans
oil the wood top of a table
then a nearby counter
put the dishes away
the keyboard at lunch
catches my eye
and my fingers spell out my dilemma
staying hopeful in the ordinary
of today.

Mornings since the fire

The squirrels dance across the fence
staying high on the narrow edge
on their tightrope to the waiting trees
far from the reach of our dog's teeth
hearing their barks
as a waste of dog breath
they can ignore.

I watch the pair of robins
newly arrived
having made our garden theirs
darting and hopping
through the garden boxes
finding their meals of bugs
knowing the dogs cannot go there
so safe this hunting ground is
they have found.

Each morning
I feed nuts to the blue jay family
our neighbor's fig tree holds their nest
filled with eggs
then their babies now fledging
they sit watching their parents gather
mouths and eyes wide open
waiting for each morsel
to be served from their parents' beaks.

All are safe and secure
in our yard
their lives unfolding
since their homes in hills sadly burned down
so thankfully I watch my backyard
become a wildlife sanctuary.

Dream

First I am trying to get a donkey
to let go of my truck
when the truck turns into a horse
with the donkey still attached
when suddenly the donkey it turns
into a cat sinking its deep claws
into my wrist and hand
when I awake
trying to avoid the cat's sharp teeth
just at the moment of what will be
a very painful bite.

I get up to take a pee
nearly trip over my dog
there in the dark of the floor
and in the bathroom's light
I discover it was all a dream
except the trip.

Space

Implied not in use
so it is assumed empty
instead it may reveal
an expanse so full
a place so rich
beyond description
and yet the message is
completely visible.

Each day

now minute to minute
every fiber of my soul
tells me to go out
fear can be overcome
uncertainties faced
change can be good

Lines

Writing poems
my therapy
the lines become
my best friends.

And there were two

The two of them
now one
on their balcony
all decked out for the evening
surveying what surrounds them
the old memories of her childhood
old friends and familiar places
that sent her into a new world
success, family and career
for him, a new landscape
spreads out ready
waiting for his creativity
no snow or chimneys
the warmth of sunshine
the cool of an evening breeze
and a life of new projects to do
for himself and his honey.

Tonight we share the bounty of their life
enjoying the sights
savoring the flavors and feelings of
this good life they have come to.

Not so much anymore

For so long I wanted to belong
to be like them
now, not so much.

Making jokes
the children don't understand
rather than explain or apologize
they laugh
ignoring the pain in the children's eyes
a look that I cannot overlook
not so much anymore.

Most would consider my stabs of pain minor
even I must admit they are petty
so I have another sip of wine
enjoy the gentle kiss of the breeze on my cheeks
count the stars as they twinkle into view
and consider myself lucky
to be me
not like them
much anymore.

Dogs' eyes

They watch me out of love
just for who I am
my successes and my failings
no judgment filters their gaze
I am who and what I am
and they love me anyway.

Patio

The wine sweetens the sour
in my mouth
the ache in my heart.

I realize I am not alone
the Moon and Stars
rise above
moving in a dark night's black
encouraging me
to do the same.

Camping

The wind has settled in for the night
blowing all afternoon must be tiring
the fire newly hatched from
a combination of twigs, branches
pine needles and matches
crackles at my back
its warmth a welcome reprieve
from the calm chill
accompanying the darkness.

A camping poem comes to my mind
and dances out the ends of my fingers
as the fires smoke chases me
to a different seats
breaking my reverie
finding cleaner breathes
my chair now invites a surprise
a view of the lake at dusk
so ends my day.

Parenthesis

My name is
almost a member
listed late
just because
so as not to be left out
again
yet I am.

Roses

Roses in the morning
opening all dewy moist
in the early mist
I admire each bloom
sweetly scented
revealing the abundance of creation
there in my garden
as is their nature

Some selected
brought into my house
to improve
they brighten the days
sweeten the evening meals
giving all they have
as time decays
petal by petal
dropping to the table
as is their nature

Roses in the vase
within days
have lost
their brilliance
fading and failing
their petals have
fallen wrinkled and cracked
as is their nature
they rest now
waiting for what comes next

Campfire

Just a slight push
to a new position
can make all the difference.

Choosing

After all the noise
they never said
not a word
nor a mean look
my gut said move
so I trusted
choosing to avoid a possibility
instead to embrace peace & goodwill
the best use of my wisdom.

Ready I am
for a bike ride in the woods
free of worry
filled with gratitude
finding peace of mind
in the wilderness.

Competition

A Stellar Jay and a Chipmunk
the unlikely pair arrive
searching out my camp
one from the air
it surveys the surrounds
with its piercing black eyes
taking in the entire scene
one head-nod at a time.

Its partner scampering
browsing every nook and cranny
a beady-eyed flash
from bench to table to open box
it searches for a prize tidbit.

Both in unison
while eager competitors
they act automatically
what is there is mine
they like us seek some bounty
believing that life offers it only to us
we resist sharing
instead of realizing it is all
part of the One
given freely to us all.

My last supper

Forgot my pillow
and the beef and
the roll of paper towels
all are waiting safely at home.

Meanwhile here in the mountains
tiring of all things turkey
the hot dogs and patties will remain
in my ice chest till
they too are safe at home
with my pillow, towels and tri tip.

Instead a cheese pizza
and a double nut-brown porter
my chosen meal
both a special prize in the Village
even better up at my camp
in the growing cool of darkness
my last night of the trip.

My last supper
in a frying pan which
warmed the pizza back to full
flavor matching the pint
all cold and frothy
straight from the bottle
now realizing
my glass is safe at home
in our picnic basket
not in my camping box.

I decide it is good thing I am
headed home in the morning
before something else is discovered forgotten.

I cannot hear my father's voice

I realized I haven't heard his voice in forty years
then the movie came on
in my head
I could not hear my father's voice
no sound or tone
it was s silent
in black and white
he played his part
he was there
his voice could not be heard.

So I wonder
did it fade
or is it just absent
now within me
like he was
mostly in my childhood?

This hole in my memories
I did miss something
the empty place reflects
what was missing
an emptiness
that has been better unnoticed
allowing me my illusions.

My question tells me
in this poem
indicates a knowing
lying dormant in me
a promise kept
for me to discover now
because I am old enough to bear it?

Being in line

She looks at me
I see her eyes
caring in that moment
she asks
she is pleasant
comfort is conveyed.

Yet I know
it will not last
it is genuine
felt
in that moment
but with so many
she cannot linger
on she goes to next
already in line.

Samuel's ice

Returning from the store
with much too much ice
a new family has camped
next to mine
I realize the extra bag of ice
is theirs.

I approach him
his apprehension
strikes me
I continue the next the seven steps
through the fear
offering my name
my hand as we grow nearer
and asking his in exchange
he relaxes
his fear is gone
and Samuel happily accepts
my gift
the bag of ice
so it did turn out to be his.

Listening

The base line is so driven
low and solid
it pounds in my heart
like the good ol' days
cross-legged
mesmerized
by the beat.

Glimpses

She doesn't visit as much now
the stairs have gone silent
I take it as a good thing
means we are doing okay
she knows it
tells me through regular glimpses
of her wings in constant motion
flitting here and there
mostly for me to remember
Dragonflies
and smile.

Breeze

I awake in the cool quiet
morning time in the mountains
one soul with binoculars
eyeing birds and distant peaks
appears in the nearby trees
a chipmunk dances by
looking for a morsel
then a gentle breeze
joins us
freshening the day
and tickling the early
dawn dew
and our cheeks.

Preparing

Town is a buzzing
early the busy bees
at work preparing
moving sweet pollen
from soul to soul
the hive is ready
open for the day.

Blowing

Pines warm in the sun
creak with each gust
warm and clear here in the forest
while above
in the atmosphere
the smoke is blowing
to the Bishop
and the Whites beyond.

Whispering

The blues echoes up the hill
drifting in my window
whispering its invitation
to come join
the Taj and Mo
Alicia and the Reverend
as they heat up the cool
making a smok'n hot evening
for us all
in the wood lot.

Notes on Sunday

I took my last hike up Cold Creek
it was so quiet during some stretches
I could only hear my own footsteps
it was peaceful and glorious.

Saying goodbye to Frank's Store
Twin Lakes Campground
his pictures on the wall and
his wife behind the cash register
hugs goodbye
we shared a few moments
how we have both changed
over the past 30 years
Rebecca's first visit to Mammoth and mine
how kids recalls Frank trying to teacher English
now the kids bring their kids to Twin Lakes
 a few years now for us both.
glorious times
summers in the mountains
for us both.

Listening is the greatest gift we can give to another human being. To be listened to, to be heard, is to know that someone else takes me seriously. That is a redemptive act. Rabbi Jonathan Sacks 2018

Last trip

Sit in line and wait
the final message
telling me to go out
be on the trail
on a better path.

The last festival here
before heading north
a different mountain high
calls me to go out
find new adventures.

The haze is clearing
my eyes can see
what my ears are telling me
let my heart lead the way
to the peaks.

Invitations

The house creaks at dawn
the dogs scratch an imagined flea
the refrigerator hums its low melody
its electric heartbeat
all invite me to start my day
to get a groove
to do what I do
the best I can.

Plan Be

I need something new
better than what has been
I am grateful and frustrated
both can and do coexist in me
responding the best way is my desire
to find a path that blends them both
into a walk that will bend me
strengthen me
give understanding.

Promises

The scent of rain is in the air
an unfulfilled promise
like a knowing glance from
stranger that begs our hopes
the clouds whisper
the breeze pending a wind
before a storm
stirs.

Second chances

Fear must be accepted
resentment released
optimism held tight
motivated by forgiveness.

Understanding

If everything continues
some form and fashion
rhyme and reason
must be there
beyond our senses.

The answers to all
questions become answers
challenges equal victory
nature is to nurture
and vice versa
all is there
beyond our senses.

Romance and fear
connect us inevitably
separation and disharmony
is the way it is supposed to be
a stew simmering til later
when its richness comes
into our mouths the following days
it become
beyond our senses.

Patience with today does not help
the blending takes too long
our bending too painful
an unknown so dark
leaves us trembling
wanting something
beyond our senses.

So understanding is all we have
in each moment
as everything continues to become
beyond our senses.

I'm no quitter

Starting out
I could not spell
phonics a mystery
unsolvable I faked it
cause I'm no quitter.

Reading a pain
only done at threat
to avoid failing
getting C's good enough
cause I'm no quitter.

The lemming effect
so as not to be a failure
to college and real textbook
undiscovered words
grammar bewildering
faking it not an option here
accepting guidance my only choice
cause I'm no quitter.

I learned how to study
reading became a must
and writing a part of the work
had to be completed to graduate
cause I'm no quitter.

Then becoming a worker
using words as healing
writing it down as proof it happened
records and reports
teaching others too
doing my spelling words
learning what they could do
the final lesson
cause I'm no quitter.

Now words flow out of me
they cannot be denied
the words are my friends
healing me
bring out what lies beneath
still unsolvable
a mystery to be discovered
cause I'm no quitter.

Confused

I understand the gravity
knowing enough physics
what revolves
is a matter of time
everything is relative
including my feelings
transforming.

Bounty

Wishing then wanting
births a desire
hunting becomes
my quest
as I search
the ups and downs
from low to high
too much at times
reveals the result
a bounty.

What am I writing for?

To notice the beauty
a Japanese maple
the cool quiet of a Fall morning
a clothesline repurposed by vines
a golden leaf falling to rest
all at work around me.

To remember life
which was
continues as a blessing
nourishing my soul
giving me wisdom
connection
in and to
the One.

To grow what heals me
the words wrap me
keeping me safe
disturbing me at times
helping me to act
to do good
to be a better me.

Bittersweet anticipation
mixed with joy and worry
brings tears to my eyes
touched like a whisper.

Dragonfly Landing

We are taking wing
Flying to a new roost
Our landing pad
Guarded by a dragonfly.

More

The landscape is changing
winter time is on the land
trees in deepest green
stand with those now bare
their color gone to the soil
to sweeten the green of their fellows
and to become the source
the soil bringing forth its own
dress of green springtime leaves.

What is gone in this time
becomes the more
of future seasons
sheltering the floor of the forest
rich umbrellas of foliage
sprouting buds
fragrant blossoms
ripening fruit juicy
strong nuts
sweet berries
the more of life.

Lights

It is dark
and the night sky is full
a glowing Moon
the twinkle of a million stars
light my way.

Secreted

I am so excited
bursting with joy
I want to tell everyone
even share the pictures
that constantly flash
my mind is electric.

Instead I must be quiet
most everyone near me
says little or nothing
so secreted my happiness remains
starved by fear
wanting to be free.

Awakening

Sunrise this morning
awoke hope and relief
opened my eyes to tasks ahead
excitement overcoming fear
and the light of a peaceful heart
the joy of the season.

Going

My mind is full
the way forward
across a churning river
each of my thoughts appear
slippery stones my only way forward
uncertain each considered step
so off-balanced as I am crossing over
makes the going tough.

Up at four
planning for what I can
not knowing my way
only a point of beginning
and one of ending
my map too open
inviting my mind
to fill it with fear
the going seems too much.

Then looking at the vision
the tightness eases
my heart fills with excitement
the unknown brightens with hopes
dreams of adventures
a newness of everyday life
a better life
the going will provide.

The rivers churning
releases my soul
my thoughts can go out
a streamside trail
comes into view
where I can tread
sure footed in this newness
even skipping down the path
becomes a possibility
and the water becomes a birthing
guiding and feeing my hope
toughing my steps
making the going much easier.

Do I fit?

Where he wonders
the awful returns
the question becomes
the answer
he knows
the truth.

The new hope
over time dissolves
left again pondering
go out
do it again
the awful drags
down against the up.

Trying so hard
then not so much
finding disappointment
in his wake
as he hopes
the tide will turn
then a few careless words
the awful strikes him down.

The sitcom turns tragic
the light fades
trapped in his seat
the awful flashes on the big screen
the drama continues.

The next minute

It is said the we only have control
of the next minute in our lives
some moments appear
the control vanishes
or was really never there.

These next minutes
a mix of expectation
and surprise
more connected to the unknown
the apparent test of reason
proves most plans
creative fiction.

It is going to be okay...
we just don't know when.
Sharon Clark, 1991

Knothole

Rebar with tile
key and dog licenses
sea glass and shells
all adorn the wood
found everywhere
and nowhere
gathered as the makings
a shelter from nature
made safe within
through a knothole
made gently
warm and cozy.

So easy

It is so easy
to get in trouble
like a kid
thinking out loud about something
when the something turns
not meaning to upset
I find myself sorry
sadly that old trapped feeling
clamps down on my neck
speechless my mouth fills
the phlegm blots out my words
silence.

Waiting

Wait I must
power is out
of my grasping hands
it slips through.

Wait I must
through sunsets and rises
blending in my eyes
revealing time passing
in my vision.

Wait I must
plans set
decisions yet to be
all churning
in my thoughts.

Wait I must
hope tangles with fear
doubt with joy
all stewing
my emotions simmering
near a boil.

And still
wait I must.

Late morning walk

On a walk before lunch
I spy a hawk
playing tag
the crows no match
uniting with its mate
the hawks soar
before diving into the lush
a creek side gulch
to search
for hip pity hop pities grazing
inviting mice munching
and hawks seeking lunch
remind me of my hunger.

My Lovely

Stretched out on a two-dog couch
the morning greets her
the house echoes
young laughter and scampering feet
everyone on his or her toes
except mysweetie
she and the dogs afloat
the couch their island of relaxation.

Morning

Prayers in the morning
amidst the clinks of coffee cups
tickled by spoons
a boy's building project
a train down the tracks
grandmother reading him a story
while grandfather eats cereal
my sweetie stretched out
releasing her tension
dogs' bellies scratched
tails all a-wag
at her fingertips touch
and me thankful
for such a good morning.

Experiences

The glow of morning
transitioned from the experiences
yesterday becomes
wisdom and uncertainty
desire and appreciation
hope and fear
acceptance and choice
all the ingredients
going out requires.

Quiet

The act of being
in the presence of others
sharing a moment
respecting privacy
theirs and mine.

Four-year-old rules

Zigzag edged knives
clearly a no no
crawling on grandparents
bare legs too ouchy
sitting on auntie's back
as she stretches
is quickly stopped
turning on the gas fireplace
again a no
so many rules
but soon each one will teach
how to get along in the world
shared by others.

Everything is fine

Offers declined
help not accepted
conversation limited
but everything is fine.

Loud voices
strained through thin lips
the appearance joy
eye contact
little to none
designed to avoid connection
that would reveal tension
so everything is fine.

We share the house
play with the boy
cook and eat
wash dishes
the required parallel play
in the adult sandbox of life
so everything is fine.

Wings

The morning breeze rouses
reminding me
the wings are flying off
missed last year
my limb broken
healed
now ready
I want to fly
off on a route
to stretch my wings.

Wanting my mind blown
seeking more in my rebirth
the sound and sight
thousands taking flight
a dawn sky crowded out
by the daily rebirth
off they go in a burst of wings
draws me to rise.

Taking flight
what they know
instinct at the helm
my knowing must be chosen
a few opportunities from the many
fill my mind's eye
crowding out the clear blue sky
so deciding what to seek
without knowing
becomes my stretch
my wings.

Can we keep

Can we keep
the phrase of the morning
believing in this day of lies
questioning everyone
everything in chaos
the wall has replaced
the last adult in the room.

Sixty-seven

I want someone to play with
and I am new here
so don't know the places
most others are already playing
so whether you're
sixty-seven or seven
it's always the same
guided only by loneliness
seeking to find places
where others are waiting
wanting someone to play with
too.

Oh

Can't see the point
except that staying busy
keeps him from seeing what
is truly important
oh, I see that is the point.

He like many does not want to notice
the white house is dark
except for the glow of his screen
he tweets out his fear
desperate to rally a base
that is baseless
unless it has an other
to hate and blame
to make themselves feel better.

They believe it is no longer important
unless it holds the promise
of profit
the so-called protective agency
wants to tear the bear's ear
from one end to another
to make a buck
for the entitled rich
their ideals measured
only in dollar signs.

The only point to finding right and better
is now measured by decimal points
the ledger book is all that counts.

Other selections from this author:

Because of a Great Longing

In Someone Else's Skin

Drops of Nothing

What's in a Year

ABOUT THE AUTHOR

I am a retired social worker. My life's work has fit me perfectly and been a good ride. I have learned much from all the people I have had the privilege to know. Whether as a utility worker at a juvenile probation ranch or a team member at a mental health inpatient unit or a clinical director at an international adoption agency; it has been an honor to serve others no mater what my station. These relationships have molded me into the person I am. It is what is shared through relationship that enables us all to become the people we were always meant to be. These recent poems were written during my last year practice. A time of personal becoming and sharing a healing space with the people I cared about. It was a very good year.

I now live in the Oregon countryside with my wife and our two dogs, nearby family and friends.